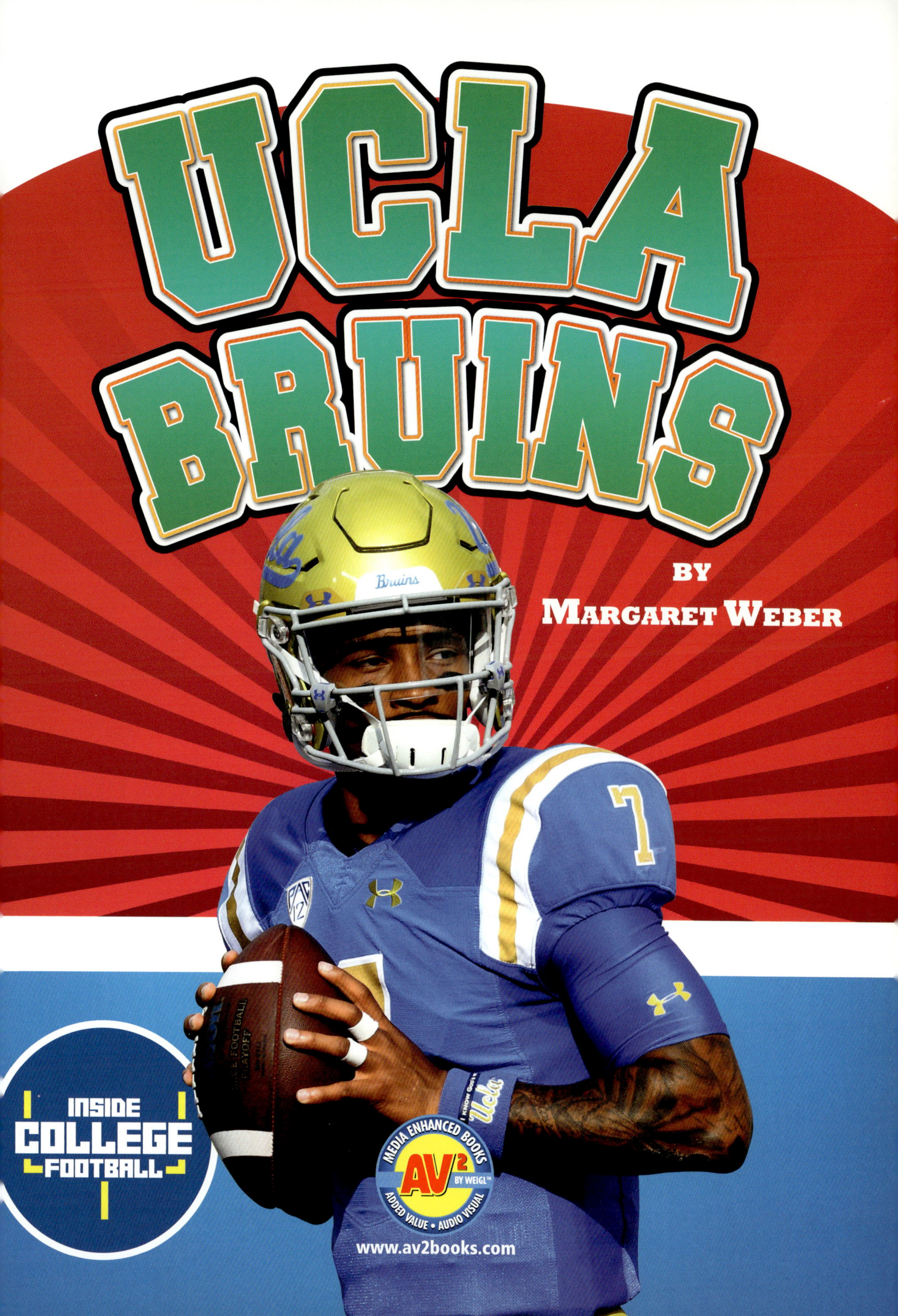
UCLA
BRUINS
BY
MARGARET WEBER
INSIDE
COLLEGE
FOOTBALL
MEDIA ENHANCED BOOKS
AV2
BY WEIGL
ADDED VALUE • AUDIO VISUAL
www.av2books.com

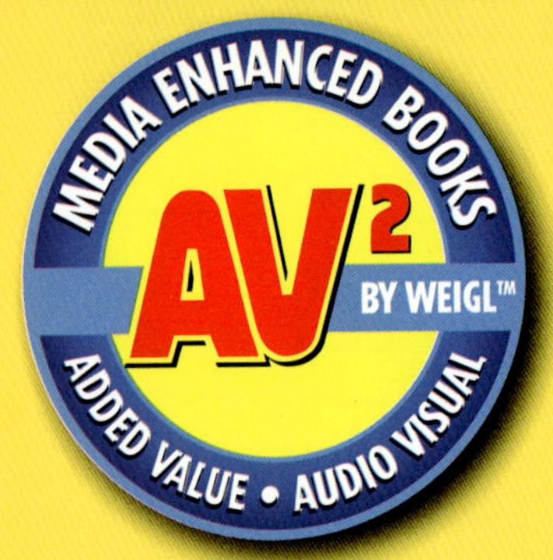

Go to www.av2books.com, and enter this book's unique code.

BOOK CODE

AVW84277

AV² by Weigl brings you media enhanced books that support active learning.

AV² provides enriched content that supplements and complements this book. Weigl's AV² books strive to create inspired learning and engage young minds in a total learning experience.

Your AV² Media Enhanced books come alive with...

Audio
Listen to sections of the book read aloud.

Key Words
Study vocabulary, and complete a matching word activity.

Video
Watch informative video clips.

Quizzes
Test your knowledge.

Embedded Weblinks
Gain additional information for research.

Slideshow
View images and captions, and prepare a presentation.

Try This!
Complete activities and hands-on experiments.

... and much, much more!

Published by AV² by Weigl
350 5th Avenue, 59th Floor
New York, NY 10118
Website: www.av2books.com

Library of Congress Control Number: 2018968227

ISBN 978-1-7911-0141-1 (hardcover)
ISBN 978-1-7911-0142-8 (multi-user eBook)
ISBN 978-1-7911-0143-5 (single-user eBook)

Printed in Guangzhou, China
1 2 3 4 5 6 7 8 9 0 23 22 21 20 19

042019
102318

Project Coordinator: Jared Siemens   Designer: Terry Paulhus

Every reasonable effort has been made to trace ownership and to obtain permission to reprint copyright material. The publishers would be pleased to have any errors or omissions brought to their attention so that they may be corrected in subsequent printings.

The publisher acknowledges Alamy, Getty Images, and Wikimedia Commons as its primary image suppliers for this title.

UCLA Bruins

CONTENTS

Introduction

The University of California, Los Angeles (UCLA) is represented in the National Collegiate Athletic Association (NCAA) by the Bruins. The Bruins play college football as part of the Pacific-12 (Pac-12) Conference. The Bruins are one of several college football teams that call California home. California football teams are known for their local **rivalries**. The Bruins' main rivals are the University of Southern California (USC) Trojans and the Golden Bears from the University of California (UC), Berkeley.

Fans of the Bruins often see their favorite players move on to professional careers. The Bruins have had 36 players chosen in the first round of the National Football League (NFL) **draft**. There have been many memorable eras of Bruins football. For example, between 1991 and 1998, the Bruins won every game against the Trojans. It was the longest winning streak for the Bruins in the history of the rivalry. Although the team has struggled in recent seasons, a new head coach and a winning spirit will lead the Bruins into the future.

Wide receiver Demetric Felton scored his first touchdown for the Bruins in a 2018 game versus the University of Arizona on a 25-yard pass. Felton played in 12 games and made eight starts for UCLA in 2018.

Running back Joshua Kelley ran for 1,243 yards during the 2018 season, the 10th most single-season yards in UCLA history.

UCLA

Stadium The Rose Bowl

Division Pacific-12 (Pac-12) South

Head Coach Chip Kelly

Location Los Angeles, California

National Championships 0

Nicknames Bruins, UCLA

1
Heisman Memorial Trophy Winner

10
Retired Jersey Numbers

36
Bowl Appearances

321
NFL Draft Picks

History

The UCLA Bruins' only **perfect season** was in 1954, when they finished with a 9–0 record.

From 1949 to 1957, under the leadership of Head Coach Henry Sanders, the Bruins had eight winning seasons and played in the Rose Bowl twice.

The first season of Bruins football was played in 1919. They joined their first conference, the Southern California Intercollegiate Athletic Association, in 1920. During the early years, the team first played high school teams, and later, other California-based teams. In 1925, William H. Spaulding became coach. He led the team to 72 wins before he left in 1938.

During the 1950s and 1960s, the Bruins built on their early years to become a national force in college football. Between 1953 and 1965, the Bruins were conference champions or co-champions six times. In 1959, they left the Pacific Coast Conference and joined the Pacific-10 Conference. The Pacific-10 Conference became the Pac-12 in 2011 and is still home to the Bruins today.

The Bruins have had many standout achievements since their early years. Players such as Gary Beban are still remembered by fans today. Beban was the first Bruins player to win a Heisman Memorial Trophy. The Bruins have 10 players who are in the Rose Bowl **Hall of Fame**. However, the team is still searching for greater achievements. They have yet to win a National Championship. The chance to make history is still possible for the Bruins.

In 1965, their first season under Coach Tommy Prothro, the Bruins completed the season with an overall 8–2–1 record and a Rose Bowl win against Michigan State University.

The Stadium

The Rose Bowl is the 15th-largest stadium in the world. Although the seating capacity is slightly more than 91,000, a record 106,869 people attended the 1973 Rose Bowl game.

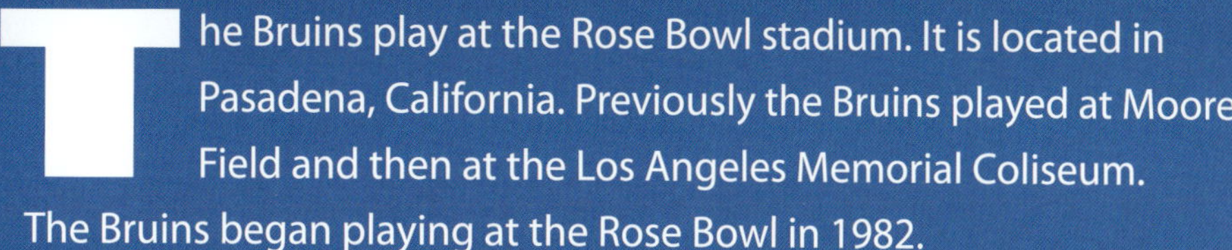

The Bruins play at the Rose Bowl stadium. It is located in Pasadena, California. Previously the Bruins played at Moore Field and then at the Los Angeles Memorial Coliseum. The Bruins began playing at the Rose Bowl in 1982.

The Rose Bowl is a **National Historic Landmark**. The stadium was dedicated on January 1, 1923, at a game between USC and Pennsylvania State University. The Rose Bowl hosted portions of the 1932 and 1984 Olympic Games. It is famous for hosting the Rose Bowl game, one of the most-watched college football games every year.

The Rose Bowl was originally a horseshoe-shaped stadium. In 1928, a **renovation** enclosed the southern end to make it a true bowl shape. There are rose bushes planted outside the entrance to welcome fans and spectators. Today, the official capacity of the stadium is 91,136. However, there are many games during which fan attendance exceeds 100,000. Watching a football game at the Rose Bowl is an exciting experience for UCLA fans.

The Rose Bowl takes its name from the Tournament of Roses Parade, which has been held on or around New Year's Day every year since 1890.

Where They Play

Welcome to The Rose Bowl, home of the UCLA Bruins. It is one of the most famous sports landmarks in the world and hosts one of college football's best-known bowl games. The Bruins play home games at the Rose Bowl, where fans surround the field in a sea of blue and gold. The Solid Gold Sound marching band plays as the team takes the field. The Bruins are ready to play.

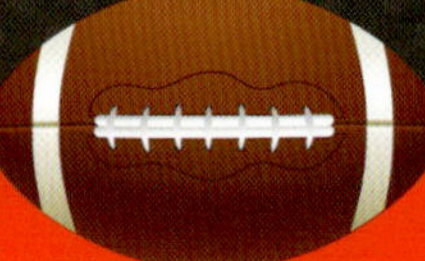

PAC-12 NORTH

1. **Oregon State University**
   Corvallis, Oregon
2. **Stanford University**
   Stanford, California
3. **University of California**
   Berkeley, California
4. **University of Oregon**
   Eugene, Oregon
5. **University of Washington**
   Seattle, Washington
6. **Washington State University**
   Pullman, Washington

Arena
The Rose Bowl

Location
Pasadena, California

Broke Ground
1922

Completed
October 1922

Surface
Real Grass

Features
- LED scoreboard is 30 feet (9 meters) high by 77 feet (23 m)
- The Court of Champions lists Rose Bowl records on the south end of the stadium
- Bricks with donor names form a rose in the plaza outside the stadium

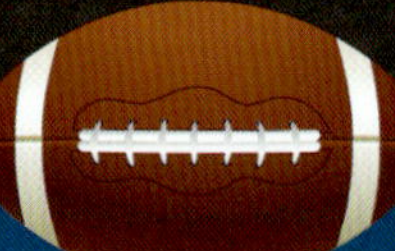

PAC-12 SOUTH

1. **Arizona State University**
   Tempe, Arizona
2. **University of Arizona**
   Tucson, Arizona
3. ★ **University of California, Los Angeles**
   Los Angeles, California
4. **University of Colorado**
   Boulder, Colorado
5. **University of Southern California**
   Los Angeles, California
6. **University of Utah**
   Salt Lake City, Utah

WASHINGTON
MONTANA
NORTH DAKOTA
WISCONSIN
OREGON
IDAHO
SOUTH DAKOTA
MINNESOTA
WYOMING
IOWA
NEVADA
NEBRASKA
UTAH
COLORADO
KANSAS
MISSOURI
CALIFORNIA
ARIZONA
OKLAHOMA
ARKANSAS
NEW MEXICO
Pacific Ocean
TEXAS
LOUISIANA
SCALE
0 miles
500 miles
0 kilometers
500 km
LEGEND
Home Stadium
Pac-12 North
Pac-12 South
United States
Other Countries
Water

The Uniforms

The **gold helmets** are the only part of the Bruins uniform that shows the UCLA logo.

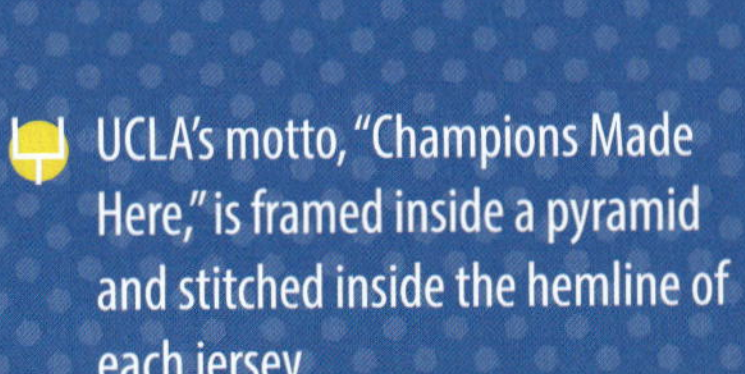

UCLA's motto, "Champions Made Here," is framed inside a pyramid and stitched inside the hemline of each jersey.

The Bruins' colors are "true blue" and gold. True blue is a shade of blue that is darker than powder blue, yet not as dark as royal blue. The true blue color was adopted by UCLA in 2003. The color was created by Adidas and the university's athletic department.

HOME

UCLA's uniforms have gone through several changes over the team's history. In 1949, a powder blue uniform was adopted, using white lettering instead of gold. Then, in the 1980s, the football team began to wear royal blue and orange uniforms that looked better on televised games. Today, the team has an all-white away uniform that has true blue lettering with gold stripes. At home, the team plays in true blue jerseys with gold letters and gold pants.

AWAY

Before UCLA launched its true blue campaign in 2003, the Bruins played in multiple shades of blue throughout the team's history, many of which resembled the colors of other schools' teams. True blue is unique to UCLA and was branded as the official color of the university.

Student Athletes

In 2010, UCLA developed a **mentor program** that pairs new student athletes with **experienced players** to support them as they start college.

Running back Joshua Kelley played two seasons at the University of California, Davis before transferring to UCLA. During the 2018 season, Kelley ran for the 10th-most yards in UCLA history and had six 100-yard rushing games. He was also on the Athletic Director's Academic Honor Roll during the 2018 season.

Being a college student athlete is hard work. Student athletes have to perform well on the football field and in the classroom. UCLA student athletes are required to meet a minimum grade point average and attend all of their classes. They must also have 12 academic credits per term. The Bruin Student-Athlete Development Program is part of the student athlete experience at UCLA. It helps all players find success after they graduate, even if they do not continue to pursue an athletic career.

Many student athletes are given athletic scholarships. An athletic scholarship is a financial aid agreement between the athlete and the college or university. Athletes who do not receive an athletic scholarship can also be "walk-on" members of the team. This means they are on the team, but without athletic financial aid. UCLA typically awards the maximum number of football scholarships allowed, which is 85.

True freshman Kazmeir Allen was mentored on the field by a fellow running back, junior Bolu Olorunfunmi, who encouraged Allen to use his gifts of speed and strength to improve his game. Allen saw action in nine games during his first season with the Bruins.

Bowl Games

Neither team scored in the first three quarters of the **1943 Rose Bowl**, the UCLA Bruins' first bowl game.

The Bruins met the Kansas State University Wildcats in the 2015 Valero Alamo Bowl. Both teams had identical records, 9–3, with the Wildcats favored to win, but the Bruins took the bowl 40–35.

Bowl games are a unique sports **tradition** in college football. In the beginning of college football, there was no true **postseason**. Today, a variety of postseason bowl games are played. Bowl games give teams the opportunity to continue striving for recognition and victory after the end of regular play. There are currently 40 bowl games played in various combinations each year. These games are chosen with input from teams, sponsors, and the College Football Playoff Selection Committee. The game **matchups** are announced in December.

The first time the Bruins competed in a bowl game was the 1943 Rose Bowl. Between 1943 and 1976, the Bruins competed in the Rose Bowl seven times and did not participate in any other bowl games. The longest winning streak for the Bruins in bowl games was between 1983 and 1991. They appeared in and won eight bowl games during that time. UCLA has an overall bowl record of 16–19–1.

UCLA made its Cactus Bowl debut in 2017. Despite a strong first half, the Bruins fell to the Wildcats 35–17.

The Coaches

Terry Donahue has the most **conference championships** in Bruins history, with a total of five titles.

In Chip Kelly's first season with the Bruins, they broke a three-game losing streak against rival University of Southern California, defeating the Trojans 34–27.

There have been 17 head coaches in Bruins history. The team's first coach was Fred Cozens, who only stayed for one year. Since then, the Bruins have been coached by some of the best college coaches in history, such as William H. Spaulding. A few coaches have made impacts that are still felt by Bruins players and fans today.

HENRY RUSSELL SANDERS Henry Sanders is remembered as the coach who made the Bruins a nationally recognized football team. He led the team to 66 wins during his **tenure** coaching the Bruins between 1949 and 1957. Sanders was responsible for changing the Bruins' uniforms to the powder blue color the team kept until 2003. Sanders also famously said, "Beating [USC] is not a matter of life and death. It's more important than that."

TERRY DONAHUE In 1976, Terry Donahue became head coach after serving as assistant coach for the team. As head coach, Donahue compiled the winningest record in Bruins history, with 151 wins. He also led the team to seven consecutive bowl wins between 1982 and 1988, which included three Rose Bowl wins. Donahue retired from the Bruins, and coaching, in 1995.

CHIP KELLY Chip Kelly is a strong coach who has coached both college and NFL teams. He joined the Bruins' coaching staff in 2017 and officially coached his first season at UCLA in 2018. Kelly coached the Philadelphia Eagles and the San Francisco 49ers before going to UCLA. Kelly was also an ESPN college football **analyst** before being hired as the Bruins' head coach. He is looking ahead to make his mark during a time of transition for UCLA's football program.

The Mascot

Joe Bruin has been a finalist for National Mascot of the Year four times. Joe is an official member of the UCLA Spirit Squad and has his own Twitter and Facebook accounts.

The mascot that represents the Bruins is Joe Bruin. Joe is a brown bear. He is often accompanied by a female brown bear named Josephine Bruin. Both Joe and Josephine Bruin are costumed mascots dressed in Bruins uniforms. They have been a part of the team since the 1960s. Before that, the university sometimes used live bears for the entertainment of the crowd.

The Bruins were known by a few different nicknames before 1926. Originally known as the Cubs, UCLA became the Grizzlies in 1924. However, they were forced to change their nickname again in 1926 when they joined the Pacific Coast Conference, which was already home to the University of Montana Grizzlies. UC Berkeley was known as both the Bruins and the Bears at that time. UC Berkeley voted to let UCLA become the Bruins, while it remained the Bears.

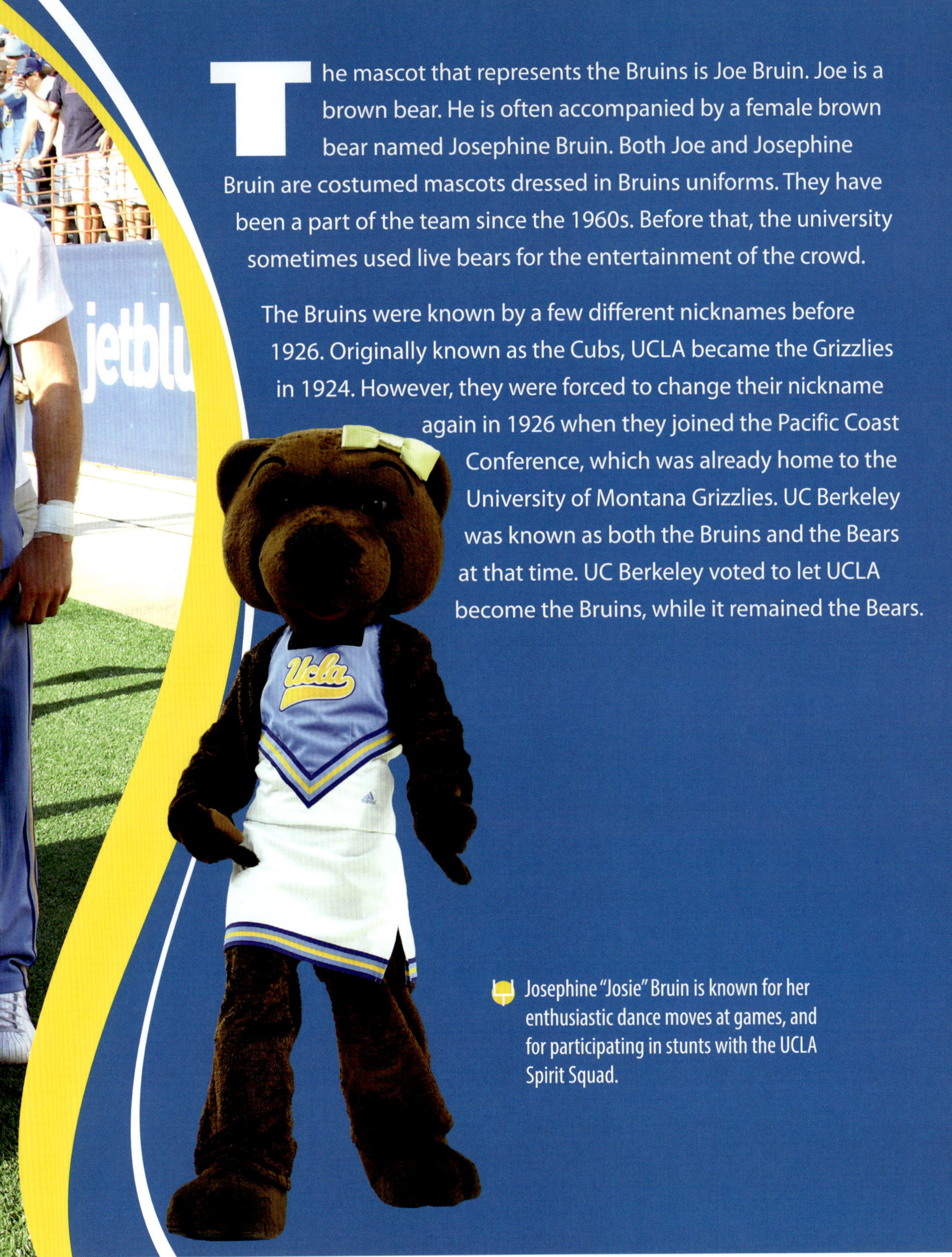

Josephine "Josie" Bruin is known for her enthusiastic dance moves at games, and for participating in stunts with the UCLA Spirit Squad.

Legends of the Past

For many players, their time with the Bruins is the start of a promising football career. These are some of the best-known football players to play for the University of California, Los Angeles.

Takkarist McKinley

Takkarist McKinley began his college football career at Contra Costa College. He transferred and began playing with the Bruins after one season. During his junior year in 2015, he started 12 of 13 games. McKinley was a strong player for the Bruins, continuing to help the team win even after he suffered a shoulder injury. McKinley's shoulder was repaired in 2017, and he was drafted by the Atlanta Falcons in the first round of the NFL draft. He remains a key player in the Falcons' defensive line.

Position: Defensive End
Seasons: 2013 (Contra Costa College), 2014–2016 (UCLA Bruins), 2017–Present (Atlanta Falcons)
Born: November 2, 1995, Oakland, California

Eric Kendricks

Eric Kendricks was not the first in his family to play for the Bruins. His father, Marvin Kendricks, was a running back for the team. Kendricks was recruited to the Bruins in 2010. During his sophomore year, he started 14 games. He also led the Pac-12 Conference in tackles for the season. During his senior year, Kendricks set a school record. He had 481 career tackles, the highest in Bruins history. Today, he plays with the NFL's Minnesota Vikings.

Position: Linebacker
Seasons: 2010–2014 (UCLA Bruins), 2015–Present (Minnesota Vikings)
Born: February 29, 1992, Clovis, California

Kenny Clark

Kenny Clark had a strong start during his time at UCLA. He started all 13 games during his freshman year in 2013. In both his sophomore and junior years, Clark was awarded All-Pac-12 honors. In 2015, he was the only player on the Bruins to receive such an honor. Clark showed his value during the Foster Farms Bowl in 2015 when he made 11 tackles during the game, the highest number of single-game tackles in his career. Clark entered the NFL draft in 2016 and was chosen by the Green Bay Packers in the first round.

Position: Tackle
Seasons: 2013–2015 (UCLA Bruins), 2016–Present (Green Bay Packers)
Born: October 4, 1995, San Bernardino, California

Josh Rosen

Josh Rosen was eager to start his football career at UCLA. He enrolled in January 2015 so that he could begin practicing with the team before the season began that fall. He was the first true freshman in Bruins history to start the first game of the season. Rosen suffered a shoulder injury in 2016. After surgery and recovery, he led his team to a comeback from a 34-point deficit in the opening game of the 2017 season. In the 2018 NFL draft, the Arizona Cardinals chose Rosen as their 10th overall pick.

Position: Quarterback
Seasons: 2015–2017 (UCLA Bruins), 2018–Present (Arizona Cardinals)
Born: February 10, 1997, Manhattan Beach, California

All-Time Records

515

Single-Game Yards

Cade McNown set a school single-game record for most yards gained during the 1998 game against the University of Miami Hurricanes, with 515 yards.

24

Single-Bowl Game Points

In the 1986 Rose Bowl, Eric Ball scored 24 points against the University of Iowa, a bowl record for the Bruins.

5

Single-Game Touchdowns

In 2004, Maurice Jones-Drew made five touchdowns in a game against the University of Washington, setting a Bruins record. He tied his own record in a game against the California Golden Bears in 2005.

85

Career Field Goals

Kai Forbath made 85 of 101 field goals attempted between 2007 and 2010, the most of any UCLA Bruins player.

161

Single-Season Tackles

Jerry Robinson holds the top spot for single-season tackles, with 161 in 1978.

Timeline

Throughout the team's history, the UCLA Bruins have had many memorable events that have become defining moments for the team and its fans.

1925
William H. Spaulding comes to California from Minnesota in order to lead the Bruins.

1938
After 14 years with the Bruins, William H. Spaulding retires with a record of 72–51–8.

1954
The team that takes the field is one of the greatest in Bruins football history. It finishes the season with a perfect 9–0 record.

1900 1920 1940 1960

In 1919, the UCLA Bruins take the field for the first time as an independent team.

1943
The Bruins play in their first Rose Bowl game.

1949
Coach Henry Sanders joins the UCLA Bruins after leaving his position at Vanderbilt University.

1983–1986
The Bruins appear in and win three Rose Bowls.

1995
After 151 wins and 20 seasons with the Bruins, Coach Donahue retires from his head coaching position.

The Future
With the arrival of Coach Kelly, the Bruins are looking ahead to a new era of college football at the university. They hope to build on their recent successes as they continue to compete in the Pac-12 Conference. Players such as Josh Rosen have made watching Bruins football exciting for fans. The Bruins hope to carry this excitement into the coming seasons.

The season opener of 2017 sees the Bruins come back from a 34-point deficit to win, setting the record for the largest comeback in Bruins history.

1980 | 2000 | 2020

1996
Coach Sanders is inducted into the College Football Hall of Fame, demonstrating his importance in Bruins and college football history.

2003
Coach Karl Dorrell comes to Pasadena to help revive the Bruins after a series of disappointing seasons.

Write a Biography

Life Story

A person's life story can be the subject of a book. This kind of book is called a biography. Biographies often describe the lives of people who have achieved great success. These people may be alive today, or they may have lived many years ago. Reading a biography can help you learn more about a great person.

Get the Facts

Use this book, and research in the library and on the internet, to find out more about your favorite player. Learn as much about him as you can. What position does he play? What are his statistics in important categories? Has he set any records? Also, be sure to write down key events in the person's life. What was his childhood like? What has he accomplished off the field? Is there anything else that makes this person special or unusual?

Use the Concept Web

A concept web is a useful research tool. Read the questions in the concept web on the following page. Answer the questions in your notebook. Your answers will help you write a biography.

Concept Web

Adulthood

- Where does this individual currently reside?
- Does he have a family?

Your Opinion

- What did you learn from the books you read in your research?
- Would you suggest these books to others?
- Was anything missing from these books?

Childhood

- Where and when was this person born?
- Describe his parents, siblings, and friends.
- Did he grow up in unusual circumstances?

Accomplishments off the Field

- What is this person's life's work?
- Has he received awards or recognition for accomplishments?
- How have this person's accomplishments served others?

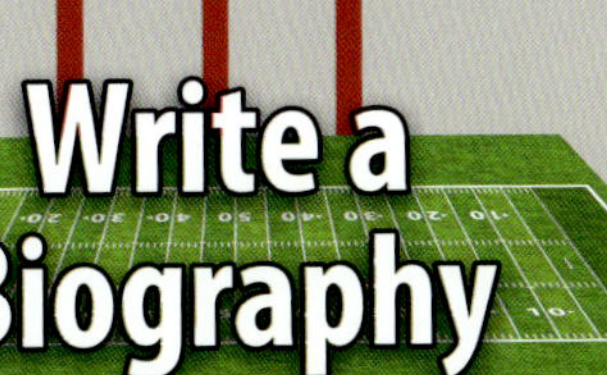

Help and Obstacles

- Did this individual have a positive attitude?
- Did he receive help from others?
- Did this person have a mentor?
- Did this person face any hardships?
- If so, how were the hardships overcome?

Accomplishments on the Field

- What records does this person hold?
- What key games and plays have defined his career?
- What are his stats in categories important to his position?

Work and Preparation

- What was this person's education?
- What was his work experience?
- How does this person work?
- What is the process he uses?

Trivia Time

Take this quiz to test your knowledge of the UCLA Bruins. The answers are printed upside down under each question.

1 How many Bruins players have been chosen in the first round of the NFL Draft?

A. 36

2 When was the longest winning streak for the Bruins against their rivals the USC Trojans?

A. Between 1991 and 1998

3 How many jersey numbers has UCLA retired?

A. 10

4 Who became coach of the Bruins in 1925?

A. William H. Spaulding

5 In which year did the Bruins play a perfect season?

A. 1954

6 Where do the Bruins play their home games?

A. The Rose Bowl stadium

7 What is the official capacity of the Rose Bowl stadium?

A. 91,136

8 What are the team's colors?

A. True blue and gold

9 Who set the single-game record for most yards gained in Bruins history?

A. Cade McNown

10 How many wins did Henry Sanders have?

A. 66

Key Words

analyst: a person whose job is to examine something

draft: an annual event where the NFL chooses college football players to be new team members

Hall of Fame: a group of persons judged to be outstanding in a particular sport

matchups: contests between two athletes or sports teams

National Historic Landmark: a site that is recognized by the United States government for its historical significance

postseason: a sporting event that takes place after the end of the regular season

renovation: construction that works to improve or expand an older building

rivalries: competitions between different groups or individuals toward the same objective or goal

tenure: the amount of time that someone holds a job

tradition: a custom or belief that is passed from one generation to another

Index

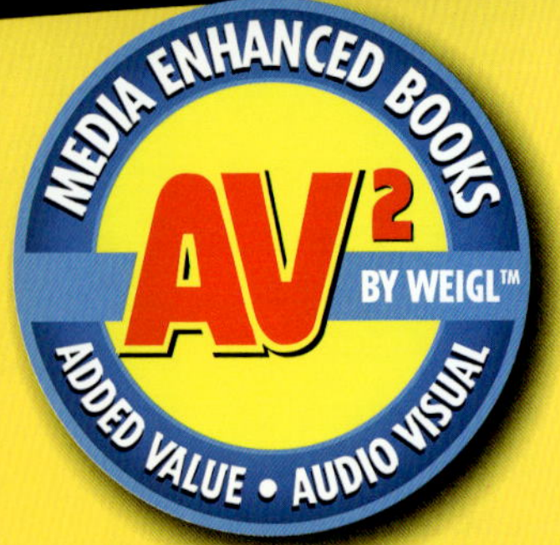

Log on to www.av2books.com

AV² by Weigl brings you media enhanced books that support active learning. Go to www.av2books.com, and enter the special code found on page 2 of this book. You will gain access to enriched and enhanced content that supplements and complements this book. Content includes video, audio, weblinks, quizzes, a slideshow, and activities.

AV² Online Navigation

Audio
Listen to sections of the book read aloud.

Book Pages
AV² pages directly correspond to pages in the book.

Video
Watch informative video clips.

Embedded Weblinks
Gain additional information for research.

Key Words
Study vocabulary, and complete a matching word activity.

Try This!
Complete activities and hands-on experiments.

Quizzes
Test your knowledge.

Slideshow
View images and captions, and prepare a presentation.

AV² was built to bridge the gap between print and digital. We encourage you to tell us what you like and what you want to see in the future.

Sign up to be an AV² Ambassador at www.av2books.com/ambassador.

Due to the dynamic nature of the internet, some of the URLs and activities provided as part of AV² by Weigl may have changed or ceased to exist. AV² by Weigl accepts no responsibility for any such changes. All media enhanced books are regularly monitored to update addresses and sites in a timely manner. Contact AV² by Weigl at 1-866-649-3445 or av2books@weigl.com with any questions, comments, or feedback.